# Alternate History

*What If?*

David Reece

Kindred Souls Press
Baytown, Texas 77520

# Prologue

Welcome to the World of "Alternate History"

History is full of pivotal moments that have shaped the world we live in today. But what if things had gone differently? What if key events had unfolded in unexpected ways? Welcome to "Alternate History: What If?", a journey through time where we explore fifteen of these moments and imagine how different our world could be if history had taken another path.

In this book, we'll dive into imaginative reimaginings of historical events, blending facts with creative possibilities. Whether it's dinosaurs still roaming the Earth, or the Roman Empire never falling, each chapter will transport you to a world of endless possibilities.

The Power of Pivotal Moments

Pivotal moments are the turning points in history that have the power to change everything. They are the events that set the course of our world, influencing everything from politics to culture, technology to daily life. By exploring these moments, we can better understand the delicate balance of history and the incredible impact of each decision and event.

Imagine if a single battle had been won or lost, a leader had made a different choice, or a natural disaster had been avoided. These moments, though sometimes small, have the potential to create ripples that affect everything. This book will help you appreciate the significance of these pivotal moments and how they shape the world we live in.

How to Use Your Imagination to Explore History

As you read through each chapter, you'll be encouraged to use your imagination. Picture yourself in the shoes of people living in these alternate worlds. Think about how their lives, their challenges, and their triumphs might be different from our own. By engaging with history in this imaginative way, you'll gain a deeper appreciation for the complexities and wonders of our past.

Don't be afraid to ask questions and let your mind wander. What would your life be like in a world where the dinosaurs never went extinct? How might technology have advanced if the Library of Alexandria had survived? Use these questions as a springboard for your imagination, allowing you to explore the endless possibilities of alternate history.

Overview of the Book's Structure

This book is divided into fifteen chapters, each focusing on a different pivotal moment in history. We'll start with ancient times and move through to the modern era, exploring a wide range of scenarios along the way. Each chapter will provide a brief overview of the actual historical event, followed by an imaginative reimagining of what could have happened if things had been different.

Here's a sneak peek at the chapters ahead:

What If the Dinosaurs Never Went Extinct?

What If the Library of Alexandria Had Survived?

What If the Roman Empire Never Fell?

What If the Black Death Had Never Occurred?

What If Christopher Columbus Hadn't Discovered America?

What If the American Revolution Had Failed?

What If Napoleon Had Won at Waterloo?

What If the South Had Won the American Civil War?

What If the Titanic Hadn't Sunk?

What If World War I Had Never Happened?

What If the Stock Market Crash of 1929 Had Been Averted?

What If World War II Had Never Happened?

What If the Space Race Had Continued?

What If the Internet Had Never Been Invented?

What If Climate Change Had Been Addressed Earlier?

Each chapter is designed to be engaging and easy to read, making complex historical concepts accessible to all readers. As you journey through these alternate histories, you'll gain new insights into the events that have shaped our world and the infinite possibilities that lie within the realm of "What If?"

# Chapter 1: What If the Dinosaurs Never Went Extinct?

Introduction to the Cretaceous Period

The Cretaceous Period, which lasted from about 145 to 66 million years ago, was the final era of the dinosaurs. It was a time of warm climates, high sea levels, and vast, lush forests. Dinosaurs ruled the land, with species ranging from the towering Tyrannosaurus rex to the gentle, long-necked Brachiosaurus. The skies were filled with flying reptiles, and the oceans teemed with marine creatures.

Life during the Cretaceous was vibrant and diverse. Flowering plants began to spread, providing new food sources for herbivorous dinosaurs. The ecosystem was complex, with a delicate balance between predators and prey. Dinosaurs had adapted to various environments, from dense forests to arid deserts, showcasing their incredible versatility.

The Asteroid That Changed Everything

Around 66 million years ago, a massive asteroid struck the Earth near what is now the Yucatan Peninsula in Mexico. This catastrophic event marked the end of the Cretaceous Period and led to the extinction of the dinosaurs. The impact released energy equivalent to billions of atomic bombs, causing wildfires, tsunamis, and a "nuclear winter" effect that drastically altered the climate.

The aftermath of the asteroid impact was devastating. Dust and debris filled the atmosphere, blocking sunlight and causing temperatures to plummet. Plants and plankton, the base of the food chain, died off, leading to the collapse of ecosystems. Within a relatively short period, about 75% of all species on Earth, including the dinosaurs, went extinct.

An Earth Still Ruled by Dinosaurs

But what if the asteroid had missed Earth, and the dinosaurs had never gone extinct? How would life on our planet be different today?

Human Evolution in a Dinosaur-Dominated World

In this alternate timeline, dinosaurs continue to thrive, evolving and adapting to the changing environment. Mammals, including early primates, still exist but must compete with dinosaurs for resources and habitats. Over millions of years, some mammals may evolve into more specialized niches, avoiding direct competition with the dominant dinosaurs.

Humans, if they evolve at all, face unique challenges. Instead of hunting large game like mammoths and bison, early humans must navigate a world where dinosaurs are both predators and competitors. They develop unique survival strategies, such as living in trees or developing advanced tools and weapons to defend themselves.

Coexistence and Conflict

In a world where humans and dinosaurs coexist, there would be constant tension and competition. Large predators like the T. rex pose a significant threat, while herbivores compete for food and territory. Humans might form small, tightly-knit communities, relying on their intelligence and cooperation to survive.

The presence of dinosaurs could also influence human culture and mythology. Stories and legends about great beasts would become integral to their societies, shaping their beliefs and traditions. Over time, humans might learn to domesticate smaller, more docile dinosaurs for labor, transportation, or companionship.

Imagining Modern-Day Dinosaur Interactions

In today's world, the existence of dinosaurs would profoundly impact our society. Imagine going on a safari to see herds of Triceratops grazing or watching Pteranodons soar above the city skyline. Zoos and wildlife parks would feature dinosaur exhibits, and paleontologists would study living specimens instead of fossils.

Technological and Environmental Impact

The presence of dinosaurs would influence technological advancements. For example, cities and infrastructure would need to be designed to withstand encounters with large, potentially dangerous animals. Transportation systems might include reinforced vehicles and elevated walkways to protect people from dinosaur encounters.

Environmental conservation efforts would also focus on preserving dinosaur habitats. Governments and organizations would work to protect these ancient creatures, balancing human development with the need to maintain natural ecosystems.

Cultural and Social Changes

Dinosaurs would become a central part of our culture, featuring prominently in art, literature, and media. They would inspire awe and fascination, becoming symbols of the ancient past and the power of nature. Education systems would include comprehensive studies of dinosaurs, and children would grow up with a deep appreciation for these incredible creatures.

In a world where dinosaurs never went extinct, our relationship with nature would be fundamentally different. We would constantly be reminded of the Earth's ancient history and the delicate balance that sustains life on our planet. This alternate history invites us to imagine a world where humans and dinosaurs share the Earth, challenging us to consider how we adapt and coexist with such magnificent creatures.

# Chapter 2: What If the Library of Alexandria Had Survived?

The Glory of Ancient Alexandria

The city of Alexandria, founded by Alexander the Great in 331 BC, was one of the most important cultural and intellectual centers of the ancient world. Located in Egypt, it became a hub for scholars, philosophers, and scientists from various cultures. The city's most renowned institution was the Library of Alexandria, established under the reign of Ptolemy I and his successors.

The Library of Alexandria was more than just a collection of scrolls; it was a symbol of knowledge and learning. It housed hundreds of thousands of documents, covering subjects such as mathematics, astronomy, medicine, literature, and philosophy. Scholars from all over the Mediterranean world came to study and share their knowledge, making it a melting pot of ideas and innovation.

The Destruction of Knowledge

The exact cause and timing of the Library's destruction are subjects of historical debate, but it is generally believed to have been destroyed in a series of events over several centuries. The loss of the Library of Alexandria represents one of the greatest intellectual tragedies of the ancient world. It resulted in the loss of countless works of art, science, and literature, many of which were irreplaceable.

The destruction of the Library had far-reaching consequences. It marked a significant setback for scientific and cultural progress. The loss of so much accumulated knowledge delayed advancements in various fields, including medicine, engineering, and astronomy. It also disrupted the transmission of ideas, leading to a period where much of the ancient wisdom was forgotten or obscured.

A World Where the Library Thrived

But what if the Library of Alexandria had survived? How would the preservation of this vast repository of knowledge have changed the course of history?

Advancements in Science and Technology

In this alternate timeline, the Library of Alexandria remains intact and continues to attract scholars from around the world. The continuous accumulation and sharing of knowledge accelerate scientific and technological advancements. Innovations that were delayed or lost due to the Library's destruction now flourish.

For example, advancements in medicine would occur much earlier. The preservation of medical texts from various cultures allows for a greater understanding of anatomy, surgery, and pharmacology. Diseases that plagued ancient societies are treated more effectively, improving overall health and longevity.

Technological developments also accelerate. Engineering principles and inventions documented in the Library lead to the creation of more advanced infrastructure, including aqueducts, roads, and buildings. The knowledge of ancient Greek and Roman engineering is preserved and expanded upon, leading to a more sophisticated and interconnected world.

Cultural and Philosophical Growth

The Library's survival also fosters a richer cultural and philosophical landscape. With access to a diverse range of texts, scholars engage in deeper and more comprehensive studies of literature, history, and philosophy. The cross-cultural exchange of ideas promotes a greater understanding and appreciation of different cultures.

Philosophical schools of thought, such as those of Plato, Aristotle, and others, thrive and evolve. The preservation of works from various traditions, including those from India, Persia, and China, enriches the intellectual discourse. This leads to the development of new philosophical frameworks that integrate different perspectives and insights.

Impact on Modern Society

Education and Literacy

The preservation of the Library of Alexandria transforms education. The continuous availability of knowledge encourages the establishment of more libraries and educational institutions. Literacy rates improve as access to books and learning materials becomes more widespread. Education systems develop with a strong emphasis on the value of knowledge and critical thinking.

Scientific and Technological Progress

By preserving ancient knowledge and fostering continuous innovation, society experiences rapid scientific and technological progress. Breakthroughs in fields such as astronomy, physics, and biology occur earlier, leading to an accelerated pace of discovery. For instance, the heliocentric model of the solar system proposed by Copernicus in the 16th century might have been realized centuries earlier.

Technological advancements also shape modern society in profound ways. The early development of complex machinery and tools leads to an industrial revolution occurring much sooner. This, in turn, impacts the economy, transportation, and communication, creating a more advanced and interconnected world.

Cultural and Social Impact

The Library's survival promotes a culture of knowledge and curiosity. Art, literature, and philosophy flourish, reflecting the diverse influences and ideas preserved in the Library. Cultural exchanges between different regions and civilizations become more common, fostering a global society that values learning and innovation.

The preservation of ancient texts also leads to a greater understanding of human history and heritage. Historical records and literary works provide insights into the lives and cultures of ancient civilizations, enriching our understanding of the past and influencing modern cultural practices.

Political and Economic Implications

The continuous accumulation and sharing of knowledge in the Library of Alexandria contribute to the stability and prosperity of the regions it influences. Enlightened leadership, informed by a deep understanding of history, philosophy, and science, guides political decisions. Economic policies benefit from advancements in technology and infrastructure, leading to increased productivity and wealth.

A Legacy of Knowledge

In this alternate history, the Library of Alexandria's survival transforms the world into a place where knowledge and innovation are highly valued. The continuous exchange of ideas and preservation of ancient wisdom accelerate scientific and cultural progress, creating a more advanced and interconnected society. By imagining a world where the Library thrived, we are reminded of the importance of preserving and sharing knowledge for the betterment of humanity.

# Chapter 3: What If the Roman Empire Never Fell?

The Rise of the Roman Empire

The Roman Empire, one of the most powerful and influential civilizations in history, began as a small city-state on the Italian Peninsula. Over centuries, it expanded its territory through military conquest, diplomacy, and strategic alliances. By the time of Emperor Augustus, around 27 BC, Rome had transformed into a vast empire encompassing much of Europe, North Africa, and parts of Asia.

The Roman Empire was known for its remarkable achievements in engineering, architecture, law, and governance. Roman roads, aqueducts, and buildings showcased advanced engineering skills, while Roman law laid the foundation for many modern legal systems. The Pax Romana, a period of relative peace and stability, allowed for economic prosperity and cultural exchange.

Factors Leading to Its Decline

Despite its greatness, the Roman Empire faced numerous challenges that ultimately led to its decline. Internal factors such as political corruption, economic troubles, and social unrest weakened the empire. External pressures from invading barbarian tribes and the rise of rival powers further strained Rome's resources and defenses.

By the late 4th and early 5th centuries, the Western Roman Empire was in a state of turmoil. The sack of Rome by the Visigoths in 410 AD marked a significant blow to the empire's prestige. The eventual deposition of the last Roman emperor in 476 AD is often cited as the end of the Western Roman Empire, though the Eastern Roman Empire, known as the Byzantine Empire, continued for nearly another thousand years.

A World Where Rome Endures

But what if the Roman Empire never fell? How would the continuation of Rome's dominance shape the world we live in today?

Global Roman Influence

In this alternate timeline, the Roman Empire successfully addresses its internal issues and repels external threats. Strong and effective leadership, along with significant reforms in governance, economy, and military, ensures the stability and longevity of the empire.

The continued existence of the Roman Empire means the spread of Roman culture, language, and governance across an even larger part of the world. Latin remains the lingua franca, facilitating communication and trade. Roman law and political structures influence the development of other nations, leading to a more unified and stable global political landscape.

Technological and Cultural Advancements

With the empire's stability, technological and cultural advancements continue to flourish. Roman engineering reaches new heights, leading to the development of advanced infrastructure such as sophisticated road networks, aqueducts, and urban planning. Innovations in architecture, such as the use of concrete and the construction of grand buildings, become even more widespread.

Culturally, the Roman Empire remains a melting pot of ideas and traditions. The preservation and enhancement of Greek and Roman knowledge lead to significant advancements in fields such as medicine, astronomy, and mathematics. The continued patronage of the arts results in a rich and diverse cultural landscape, with literature, theater, and visual arts thriving.

The Modern Roman World

Political and Economic Structures

The continuation of the Roman Empire results in a global political system influenced by Roman principles. Democratically elected senates and councils govern various regions, ensuring representation and accountability. The concept of citizenship, with its associated rights and responsibilities, becomes a cornerstone of global society.

Economically, the stability and prosperity of the Roman Empire promote international trade and commerce. The use of a common currency facilitates economic transactions, while a standardized system of weights and measures ensures fairness and consistency. The empire's vast network of roads and ports enhances connectivity, making the exchange of goods and ideas more efficient.

Social and Cultural Impact

The preservation of Roman culture and traditions shapes the social fabric of the modern world. Roman festivals, rituals, and customs continue to be celebrated, fostering a sense of continuity and shared heritage. The emphasis on public education and literacy, a hallmark of Roman society, leads to high literacy rates and a well-informed populace.

The Roman approach to religion, characterized by tolerance and the incorporation of diverse beliefs, results in a multicultural and pluralistic society. The coexistence of various religious traditions promotes mutual respect and understanding, reducing religious conflicts and fostering a more harmonious world.

Technological and Scientific Progress

The ongoing stability and prosperity of the Roman Empire create an environment conducive to scientific and technological progress. The preservation and enhancement of ancient knowledge lead to significant breakthroughs in fields such as engineering, medicine, and astronomy. For example, the understanding of hydraulics and mechanics paves the way for the development of complex machinery and tools.

Medical advancements also benefit from the continuous exchange of knowledge. The study of human anatomy, surgery, and pharmacology advances, leading to improved healthcare and increased life expectancy. The early establishment of public health systems and sanitation infrastructure contributes to overall societal well-being.

Environmental and Urban Planning

Roman urban planning principles, such as the grid layout and efficient use of space, influence modern city design. Cities are planned with an emphasis on functionality, aesthetics, and sustainability. The use of green spaces, public baths, and theaters enhances the quality of urban life, while advanced infrastructure ensures the efficient delivery of services.

Environmental conservation becomes a priority, with the preservation of natural resources and ecosystems. Roman agricultural practices, including crop rotation and irrigation, are refined and expanded, ensuring food security and environmental sustainability.

A Legacy of Rome

In this alternate history, the survival and continued dominance of the Roman Empire create a world characterized by stability, prosperity, and cultural richness. The influence of Roman principles in governance, law, and society fosters a more unified and harmonious global community. Technological and scientific advancements propel humanity forward, while the preservation of Roman culture ensures a deep appreciation for the past.

By imagining a world where the Roman Empire never fell, we gain insights into the potential of human civilization when guided by principles of knowledge, innovation, and unity. This alternate history invites us to reflect on the lessons of the past and the possibilities for the future, reminding us of the enduring impact of pivotal moments in history.

# Chapter 4: What If the Black Death Had Never Occurred?

The Devastation of the Black Death

The Black Death, also known as the Bubonic Plague, struck Europe in the mid-14th century with catastrophic consequences. Originating in Asia, the plague spread rapidly through trade routes, reaching Europe around 1347. The disease, caused by the bacterium Yersinia pestis, was transmitted through fleas that infested black rats, which were common on merchant ships.

The impact of the Black Death was profound. It killed an estimated 25-30 million people in Europe, about one-third of the population, within just a few years. The high mortality rate caused widespread panic and despair, leading to significant social, economic, and political upheaval. Entire villages were wiped out, agricultural production plummeted, and labor shortages created economic disruptions.

Europe Before the Plague

Before the arrival of the Black Death, Europe was experiencing a period of growth and relative stability. The population was increasing, and cities were expanding. Advances in agriculture, such as the three-field system, had improved food production, leading to better nutrition and higher life expectancy. Trade and commerce were flourishing, connecting Europe with distant regions and facilitating cultural exchange.

Medieval Europe was also characterized by a hierarchical social structure. The feudal system, with its rigid class divisions, dominated rural areas, while towns and cities were governed by merchant guilds and local elites. The Catholic Church played a central role in daily life, influencing education, culture, and politics. This period, known as the High Middle Ages, set the stage for the significant transformations that would follow.

A World Without the Black Death

But what if the Black Death had never occurred? How would the absence of this devastating plague have changed the course of European history and the world at large?

Population Growth and Urban Development

In this alternate timeline, Europe continues to experience population growth without the interruption of the Black Death. By the late 14th and early 15th centuries, the population is much larger than it was in our timeline. This leads to increased urbanization, as people move to cities in search of opportunities.

Cities grow and expand, becoming centers of commerce, culture, and innovation. The increased population drives demand for goods and services, stimulating economic growth. With more people living in urban areas, there is a greater focus on improving infrastructure, such as roads, bridges, and sanitation systems. The growth of cities also fosters the development of universities and centers of learning, promoting education and intellectual exchange.

Scientific and Medical Advancements

The absence of the Black Death means that Europe does not experience the same level of social and economic disruption. This stability allows for continuous progress in science and medicine. Without the distraction and devastation of the plague, scholars and physicians can focus on advancing their knowledge and developing new treatments for diseases.

The Renaissance, a period of renewed interest in classical learning and the arts, occurs earlier and more robustly. The preservation and study of ancient Greek and Roman texts lead to significant advancements in various fields, including anatomy, astronomy, and physics. The development of the scientific method is accelerated, laying the groundwork for future discoveries and innovations.

Impact on Modern Healthcare

Early Public Health Systems

In this alternate history, the absence of the Black Death encourages the development of public health systems much earlier. With a focus on preventing disease and promoting hygiene, cities implement measures such as clean water supply, waste disposal, and public baths. These early public health initiatives improve overall health and reduce the spread of infectious diseases.

The understanding of disease transmission and the importance of hygiene becomes more advanced. Physicians and scholars study the causes of illnesses and develop effective treatments, leading to a healthier population. The emphasis on public health also influences urban planning, with cities designed to minimize the risk of disease outbreaks.

Medical Innovations and Discoveries

The continuous focus on medical research and innovation results in significant breakthroughs. The study of human anatomy, aided by dissection and observation, leads to a better understanding of the body's functions and the causes of diseases. Surgical techniques improve, and the development of new instruments and methods enhances the effectiveness of medical treatments.

The discovery and use of medicinal plants and compounds are accelerated. Physicians experiment with various remedies, leading to the development of more effective treatments for common ailments. The early use of antiseptics and anesthesia revolutionizes surgery, making it safer and more successful.

Economic and Social Transformations

Feudalism and Social Mobility

The absence of the Black Death allows for a more gradual and less disruptive transformation of European society. The feudal system, with its rigid social hierarchies, evolves over time rather than collapsing abruptly. As the population grows and urbanizes, opportunities for social mobility increase. The rise of a merchant and artisan class challenges the traditional power of the nobility, leading to a more dynamic and fluid social structure.

Economic Growth and Innovation

With continuous population growth and urban development, Europe experiences sustained economic growth. The increased demand for goods and services drives innovation and the development of new technologies. The invention of the printing press, for example, occurs earlier and spreads more rapidly, facilitating the dissemination of knowledge and ideas.

Trade and commerce flourish, connecting Europe with other parts of the world. The absence of the economic disruptions caused by the Black Death allows for the continuous expansion of trade networks. This increased connectivity fosters cultural exchange and the spread of new ideas, further driving innovation and progress.

Political and Cultural Impact

Political Stability and Governance

The stability brought about by the absence of the Black Death influences the political landscape of Europe. Monarchies and governments are able to maintain control and implement reforms without the upheaval caused by the plague. This leads to more stable and effective governance, with a focus on improving infrastructure, public health, and education.

The early development of representative institutions, such as parliaments and councils, promotes political participation and accountability. The concept of the rule of law, influenced by Roman legal principles, becomes more entrenched, leading to a fairer and more just society.

Cultural Renaissance

The continuous progress in science, medicine, and the arts leads to a cultural renaissance. The study and appreciation of classical texts inspire a renewed interest in literature, philosophy, and the arts. The patronage of artists, writers, and scholars by wealthy merchants and rulers fosters a vibrant cultural scene.

The early development of universities and centers of learning promotes intellectual exchange and collaboration. Scholars fro

In this alternate history, the absence of the Black Death creates a world characterized by continuous progress and stability. The uninterrupted population growth and urban development drive economic and social transformations, while advancements in science and medicine improve overall health and well-being. The early development of public health systems and medical innovations leads to a healthier and more prosperous society.

By imagining a world without the Black Death, we gain insights into the potential for human progress when not hindered by devastating epidemics. This alternate history reminds us of the importance of public health, the value of knowledge and innovation, and the enduring impact of pivotal moments in history.

# Chapter 5: What If Christopher Columbus Hadn't Discovered America?

In 1492, Christopher Columbus, an Italian navigator sponsored by the Spanish monarchy, embarked on a voyage across the Atlantic Ocean. His goal was to find a new route to Asia by sailing westward. Instead, he landed in the Americas, opening up a new world for European exploration and colonization. This event marked the beginning of significant cultural, economic, and political changes for both Europe and the indigenous peoples of the Americas.

Columbus's discovery led to the widespread exchange of goods, ideas, and people between the Old and New Worlds, known as the Columbian Exchange. While it brought wealth and new resources to Europe, it also resulted in the devastating impact on indigenous populations through disease, warfare, and enslavement.

Native Civilizations in Pre-Columbian America

Before Columbus's arrival, the Americas were home to diverse and complex civilizations. In Mesoamerica, the Aztecs and the Maya had developed sophisticated societies with advanced knowledge of mathematics, astronomy, and architecture. The Inca Empire, located in the Andes region, was known for its remarkable engineering and administrative skills, managing vast territories through a network of roads and communication systems.

In North America, various indigenous tribes lived in harmony with their environment, each with its own unique culture, language, and social structure. The Iroquois Confederacy, for example, was a powerful alliance of six Native American tribes that practiced democratic principles and maintained a complex political system.

A World Where America Remained Undiscovered

But what if Columbus had never made his historic voyage? How would the absence of European discovery and colonization have affected the Americas and the rest of the world?

The Evolution of Native Societies

In this alternate timeline, indigenous civilizations in the Americas continue to develop and evolve without the interruption of European colonization. The Aztecs, Maya, and Inca, along with countless other tribes and nations, advance their knowledge and technologies. Trade networks expand, allowing for the exchange of goods and ideas across the continent.

Without the introduction of European diseases, the population of indigenous peoples remains robust. Cultural and intellectual achievements flourish, resulting in unique contributions to art, science, and governance. The peaceful coexistence and occasional conflicts among native societies shape a diverse and dynamic cultural landscape.

Different Colonial Powers

Although Columbus did not discover America, it is likely that other European explorers would eventually reach the New World. However, the timing and nature of their encounters with the indigenous peoples would be different. The absence of early Spanish conquest might lead to other European powers, such as the Portuguese, French, or English, becoming the primary colonizers.

The interactions between European settlers and native populations would vary based on the different colonial approaches. For instance, the French, known for their relatively cooperative relationships with Native Americans in Canada, might establish similar patterns of trade and alliance in other parts of the Americas. The Portuguese, with their experience in Brazil, might focus on different regions and resources.

Modern America in an Alternate Timeline

Political and Social Structures

In this alternate history, the political landscape of the Americas is vastly different. Indigenous nations maintain their sovereignty and governance structures, negotiating treaties and alliances with European powers. The diversity of political systems, from democratic councils to centralized empires, shapes a rich tapestry of governance.

The absence of large-scale colonization and the forced displacement of native populations result in a more integrated and multicultural society. Indigenous languages, customs, and traditions are preserved and respected, influencing the development of a unique American identity. The blending of European and native cultures creates a vibrant and diverse social fabric.

Economic Development

The economic development of the Americas follows a different trajectory in this timeline. Without the early exploitation of resources by European colonizers, indigenous societies continue to utilize sustainable agricultural practices and resource management. The introduction of new technologies and trade goods from Europe enhances local economies, leading to increased prosperity.

The absence of the transatlantic slave trade has profound implications for the economic and social development of the Americas. Without the forced labor of African slaves, societies develop alternative labor systems based on cooperation and mutual benefit. This results in a more equitable distribution of wealth and resources.

Cultural Exchange and Innovation

The ongoing exchange of ideas and technologies between indigenous peoples and European settlers fosters a rich environment of innovation. Native knowledge of agriculture, medicine, and environmental management is combined with European advancements in science and technology. This synergy leads to significant progress in various fields, including agriculture, medicine, and engineering.

Cultural exchange also influences the arts, literature, and philosophy. Indigenous storytelling, art forms, and spiritual practices inspire new genres and styles in literature and visual arts. The blending of musical traditions creates unique sounds and rhythms, enriching the cultural landscape of the Americas.

Global Implications of a Different Discovery

Impact on Europe and Asia

The delayed or altered discovery of the Americas affects the global balance of power. European nations, deprived of the immediate wealth from American resources, focus their expansion efforts on Asia and Africa. The competition for colonies in these regions intensifies, leading to different geopolitical dynamics.

The absence of the Columbian Exchange, which brought new crops and goods to Europe, affects agricultural and economic development. Without the introduction of crops like potatoes, maize, and tomatoes, European diets and farming practices remain less diverse. This impacts population growth and economic stability in Europe and Asia.

Technological and Scientific Progress

The altered course of exploration and colonization influences the development of technology and science. The absence of the American gold and silver influx affects the European economy, slowing the pace of some technological advancements. However, the continued focus on trade with Asia and Africa fosters innovation in navigation, shipbuilding, and other fields.

The exchange of knowledge between indigenous peoples and Europeans in this alternate timeline leads to different scientific discoveries. Native expertise in agriculture, medicine, and environmental management combines with European scientific methods, resulting in unique advancements and innovations.

A Different Path for Humanity

In this alternate history, the world takes a different path with Columbus never discovering America. The preservation and flourishing of indigenous civilizations lead to a richer and more diverse cultural landscape. The interactions between native peoples and European settlers shape a more equitable and cooperative society, influencing political, social, and economic development.

By imagining a world where the Americas remained undiscovered by Columbus, we gain insights into the potential for human progress when different cultures and knowledge systems are respected and integrated. This alternate history invites us to reflect on the impact of exploration and colonization, reminding us of the value of diversity, cooperation, and mutual respect in shaping our shared future.

# Chapter 6: What If the American Revolution Had Failed?

The Fight for Independence

The American Revolution, which took place between 1775 and 1783, was a monumental struggle for independence from British rule. The thirteen American colonies, motivated by a desire for self-governance and freedom from oppressive taxation, engaged in a fierce conflict with the British Empire. Key figures like George Washington, Thomas Jefferson, and Benjamin Franklin played crucial roles in the revolutionary movement, leading the colonies to victory and the eventual establishment of the United States of America.

The Declaration of Independence, signed on July 4, 1776, marked a defining moment in the revolution. It articulated the colonies' grievances against King George III and their right to self-determination. Despite early setbacks, the Continental Army, under Washington's leadership, secured critical victories, including the pivotal Battle of Saratoga in 1777 and the final victory at Yorktown in 1781, leading to the Treaty of Paris in 1783, which recognized American independence.

Key Battles and Turning Points

The American Revolution was marked by several key battles and turning points that shaped its outcome. The initial battles of Lexington and Concord in 1775 ignited the conflict, signaling the colonies' willingness to fight for their rights. The Battle of Bunker Hill, despite being a British victory, demonstrated the colonists' resilience and determination.

The harsh winter at Valley Forge in 1777-1778 tested the Continental Army's resolve, but under the training of Baron von Steuben, the troops emerged stronger and more disciplined. The French alliance in 1778, secured by Benjamin Franklin, provided crucial military support and resources, turning the tide in favor of the American cause. The final siege of Yorktown in 1781, where British General Cornwallis surrendered, effectively ended the war and secured American independence.

A World Where Britain Retained Control

But what if the American Revolution had failed, and Britain retained control over the American colonies? How would this alternate history have unfolded, and what impact would it have had on the development of the United States and the world?

The Development of British America

In this alternate timeline, the British successfully suppress the American Revolution, maintaining control over the colonies. The colonial rebellion is quashed through a combination of military might and strategic concessions. Britain imposes stricter control but also implements reforms to address some of the colonies' grievances, such as reducing taxation and increasing representation in Parliament.

The colonies remain an integral part of the British Empire, contributing to its economic and strategic strength. British America develops as a major economic power, benefiting from the empire's vast resources and trade networks. The integration of colonial and British economies leads to significant advancements in industry and commerce, fostering economic growth and prosperity.

Influence on Global Politics

The failure of the American Revolution has far-reaching implications for global politics. The absence of a successful American independence movement delays or alters the course of other revolutionary movements around the world. The French Revolution, inspired in part by the American example, may be less radical or take a different trajectory. Other colonial independence movements in Latin America and elsewhere are similarly affected, potentially leading to prolonged periods of colonial rule.

Britain's continued dominance in North America strengthens its global influence, allowing it to exert greater control over international trade and politics. The British Empire's expansion into other regions, such as Asia and Africa, may proceed with greater momentum, reshaping global geopolitics and colonial dynamics.

Modern Day Implications

Political and Social Structures

In this alternate history, British America develops its own distinct political and social structures within the framework of the British Empire. The colonies gradually gain more autonomy and representation, evolving into a semi-independent federation similar to Canada or Australia. Local governments and institutions play a significant role in governance, while still recognizing the authority of the British Crown and Parliament.

The social structure of British America reflects a blend of British and colonial influences. The class system is less rigid than in Britain, allowing for greater social mobility and economic opportunity. The continued presence of British culture and traditions influences education, law, and societal norms, creating a unique blend of British and American identities.

Economic Development and Innovation

The economic development of British America benefits from the stability and resources of the British Empire. Industrialization occurs at a rapid pace, fueled by access to raw materials and markets within the empire. The development of infrastructure, such as railways and ports, supports economic growth and facilitates trade and commerce.

Innovation thrives in this stable and prosperous environment. Scientific and technological advancements occur in various fields, including agriculture, manufacturing, and transportation. The integration of British and American expertise leads to significant breakthroughs, propelling British America to the forefront of global innovation.

Cultural Exchange and Identity

The cultural landscape of British America is characterized by a rich exchange of ideas and traditions. The blending of British and colonial cultures creates a diverse and dynamic society. Literature, art, and music reflect this cultural fusion, producing unique and influential works that shape the national identity.

The preservation of indigenous cultures and traditions is also a significant aspect of this alternate history. Without the disruptive impact of a prolonged revolutionary war, indigenous peoples maintain greater autonomy and influence. Their contributions to the cultural and social fabric of British America are recognized and respected, enriching the national identity.

Impact on International Relations

British-American Relations

The continued union of Britain and the American colonies fosters a strong and cooperative relationship. The shared economic and political interests lead to close ties and mutual support. This alliance influences international relations, with British America playing a significant role in global diplomacy and conflict resolution.

The British-American partnership also affects the balance of power in Europe and beyond. The combined economic and military strength of the two regions shapes global politics, influencing the outcomes of conflicts and negotiations. The presence of a powerful and united British Empire deters rival powers and promotes stability in international relations.

Influence on Global Independence Movements

The failure of the American Revolution has a profound impact on global independence movements. The example of a successful colonial rebellion serves as a powerful inspiration for other movements seeking self-determination. Without this precedent, the struggle for independence in various regions faces greater challenges and delays.

However, the gradual granting of autonomy and representation within the British Empire provides an alternative model for achieving self-governance. This approach influences the development of other colonial regions, leading to a more gradual and negotiated process of decolonization. The resulting political structures are more stable and integrated, reducing the likelihood of conflicts and instability.

A Different Path to Independence

In this alternate history, the failure of the American Revolution creates a world where British America remains an integral part of the British Empire. The colonies develop their own distinct identity and governance structures within the framework of the empire, benefiting from economic stability and cultural exchange. The absence of a prolonged revolutionary war fosters a more gradual and peaceful evolution of self-governance.

By imagining a world where the American Revolution failed, we gain insights into the potential for different paths to independence and self-determination. This alternate history highlights the importance of cooperation, gradual reform, and the blending of diverse cultural influences in shaping a stable and prosperous society. It reminds us that history is shaped by pivotal moments and decisions, and exploring these possibilities helps us appreciate the complexities and nuances of our shared past.

# Chapter 7: What If Napoleon Had Won at Waterloo?

Napoleon's Rise and Fall

Napoleon Bonaparte, one of history's most brilliant military leaders, rose to prominence during the French Revolution. By 1804, he had crowned himself Emperor of the French and embarked on a series of military campaigns that expanded the French Empire across much of Europe. His innovative tactics and strategic genius led to numerous victories, but his ambition also set the stage for his eventual downfall.

Napoleon's aggressive expansionism provoked a coalition of European powers determined to curb his influence. After a series of costly wars and a disastrous invasion of Russia in 1812, Napoleon's empire began to crumble. He was eventually defeated and exiled to the island of Elba in 1814. However, he escaped in 1815 and returned to power for a brief period known as the Hundred Days, culminating in his final defeat at the Battle of Waterloo.

The Battle of Waterloo

The Battle of Waterloo, fought on June 18, 1815, was a decisive confrontation between Napoleon's French army and the Seventh Coalition, led by the Duke of Wellington and the Prussian General Blücher. The battle took place near Waterloo in present-day Belgium. Despite his tactical brilliance, Napoleon faced overwhelming odds, with the Coalition forces outnumbering his own.

After a long and grueling battle, Napoleon's forces were ultimately defeated. This loss marked the end of the Napoleonic Wars and led to Napoleon's final exile to the remote island of Saint Helena, where he spent the remaining years of his life. The defeat at Waterloo reshaped the political landscape of Europe, leading to the restoration of monarchies and a period of relative peace.

A Victorious Napoleon

But what if Napoleon had won at Waterloo? How would a victory at this crucial battle have altered the course of European and global history?

Changes in European Politics

In this alternate timeline, Napoleon's victory at Waterloo solidifies his control over France and much of Europe. The Seventh Coalition is forced to negotiate peace on terms favorable to Napoleon, recognizing his authority and territorial gains. The French Empire remains a dominant power in Europe, reshaping the political landscape.

The continued presence of Napoleon's empire challenges the traditional monarchies and aristocracies of Europe. Republican ideals and revolutionary principles spread further, leading to political reforms and the establishment of more representative governments. The influence of the French legal system, including the Napoleonic Code, extends across the continent, promoting principles of equality and justice.

The Spread of Napoleonic Ideals

Napoleon's victory reinforces his role as a champion of the Enlightenment ideals of liberty, equality, and fraternity. These principles become more deeply ingrained in European society, influencing education, governance, and social structures. The promotion of meritocracy and the reduction of aristocratic privileges lead to a more dynamic and mobile society.

The spread of these ideals also affects colonial policies. The French Empire's approach to its colonies, influenced by revolutionary principles, emphasizes the integration and equal treatment of colonial subjects. This leads to the gradual abolition of slavery and the implementation of reforms that improve the rights and conditions of indigenous populations.

Modern Europe Under Napoleon's Influence

Political Structures and Governance

In this alternate history, Europe is characterized by a balance of power between the French Empire and other major nations. While Napoleon maintains control over his empire, he also fosters alliances and cooperates with other European powers to maintain stability. This leads to a more unified and cooperative Europe, with a focus on collective security and economic collaboration.

The political structures of European nations reflect a blend of Napoleonic and traditional elements. Constitutions and representative institutions become more common, influenced by the principles of the French Revolution. The spread of the Napoleonic Code standardizes legal systems, promoting fairness and justice across the continent.

Economic Development and Industrialization

Napoleon's continued reign promotes economic development and industrialization. His policies encourage infrastructure improvements, such as the construction of roads, bridges, and canals, facilitating trade and commerce. The stability provided by his rule fosters investment and innovation, leading to significant advancements in industry and technology.

The industrial revolution, already underway in Britain, spreads more rapidly across Europe. The exchange of ideas and technologies between nations accelerates progress, resulting in improved manufacturing processes, transportation systems, and communication networks. The economic integration of Europe creates a prosperous and interconnected continent.

Social and Cultural Impact

The influence of Napoleonic ideals extends to the social and cultural spheres. Education reforms, emphasizing science, mathematics, and the humanities, promote a well-rounded and enlightened citizenry. The establishment of public education systems ensures that knowledge and skills are accessible to all, regardless of social background.

Cultural exchange flourishes under Napoleon's rule. The blending of French and local traditions creates a rich and diverse cultural landscape. Art, literature, and music reflect the fusion of classical and revolutionary influences, producing innovative and influential works that shape European identity.

Global Implications of a Napoleonic Victory

Impact on Colonialism and Global Politics

Napoleon's continued dominance in Europe affects global politics and colonialism. The French Empire's approach to its colonies, based on principles of equality and integration, influences other colonial powers. Reforms in colonial governance improve the rights and conditions of indigenous populations, leading to a more equitable and humane approach to colonialism.

The balance of power in Europe, maintained by Napoleon's influence, also impacts global alliances and conflicts. European nations, focusing on cooperation and collective security, avoid the large-scale conflicts that characterized the 19th and early 20th centuries. This stability promotes international trade and diplomacy, fostering a more peaceful and interconnected world.

Technological and Scientific Advancements

The stability and prosperity provided by Napoleon's rule create an environment conducive to scientific and technological advancements.

The exchange of ideas and knowledge between European nations accelerates progress in various fields, including medicine, engineering, and the natural sciences. The establishment of research institutions and universities promotes innovation and discovery.

Technological advancements, driven by the needs of industry and infrastructure, lead to significant improvements in transportation and communication. The development of railways, steamships, and telegraph systems connects Europe and the world, facilitating the movement of people, goods, and ideas. This technological progress lays the foundation for future innovations, such as electricity and the internal combustion engine.

A Unified and Enlightened Europe

In this alternate history, Napoleon's victory at Waterloo creates a world characterized by stability, progress, and enlightenment. The principles of the French Revolution, reinforced by Napoleon's rule, shape the political, social, and cultural landscape of Europe. The emphasis on equality, meritocracy, and justice leads to a more unified and prosperous continent.

The impact of a Napoleonic victory extends beyond Europe, influencing global politics and colonialism. The spread of enlightened ideals promotes a more humane and equitable approach to governance and international relations. Technological and scientific advancements, driven by cooperation and stability, propel humanity forward, creating a brighter and more connected future.

By imagining a world where Napoleon won at Waterloo, we gain insights into the potential for human progress when guided by principles of enlightenment and cooperation. This alternate history invites us to reflect on the importance of pivotal moments and the enduring impact of visionary leadership in shaping our shared destiny.

# Chapter 8: What If the South Had Won the American Civil War?

The Causes and Course of the Civil War

The American Civil War, fought from 1861 to 1865, was a defining conflict in United States history. It arose primarily from the deep-seated issue of slavery and states' rights. The southern states, forming the Confederate States of America, sought to preserve their way of life, which relied heavily on enslaved labor. The northern states, known as the Union, aimed to preserve the nation and eventually abolish slavery.

Key battles such as Gettysburg, Antietam, and Bull Run marked the brutal and costly nature of the war. Leaders like President Abraham Lincoln and General Ulysses S. Grant in the North, and President Jefferson Davis and General Robert E. Lee in the South, played crucial roles in shaping the strategies and outcomes of the conflict. The Union's victory at the Battle of Gettysburg in 1863 and the eventual capture of Richmond in 1865 were pivotal in securing the North's triumph.

Key Battles and Strategies

The Civil War featured numerous significant battles and military campaigns that determined its outcome. The Battle of Fort Sumter in 1861 marked the war's beginning, signaling the South's willingness to secede and fight for its independence. The Battle of Antietam in 1862, the bloodiest single-day battle in American history, provided the Union with a strategic advantage and the opportunity for President Lincoln to issue the Emancipation Proclamation.

The Siege of Vicksburg in 1863 divided the Confederacy and gave the Union control of the Mississippi River, while the Battle of Gettysburg, also in 1863, was a turning point that halted General Lee's invasion of the North. The Union's strategic use of railroads, superior industrial capacity, and effective naval blockades contributed significantly to their eventual victory.

A Confederate Victory

But what if the South had won the American Civil War? How would a Confederate victory have shaped the course of American history and its impact on the world?

Social and Economic Impact

In this alternate timeline, the Confederacy successfully defends its territory and negotiates a peace treaty with the Union, leading to the establishment of two separate nations: the Confederate States of America and the United States of America. The Confederate victory solidifies the institution of slavery, delaying its abolition and perpetuating a system of racial inequality and oppression.

The Southern economy, heavily reliant on agriculture and enslaved labor, continues to dominate. However, the lack of industrialization hampers long-term economic growth and development. The North, with its industrial base and infrastructure, advances more rapidly, creating an economic disparity between the two nations.

Political and International Relations

The political landscape of North America is drastically different. The Confederate States, built on principles of states' rights and limited central government, face internal conflicts and challenges to national unity. The United States, on the other hand, continues to evolve as a federal republic with a stronger central government.

Internationally, the Confederate victory has significant implications. European powers, particularly Britain and France, recognize the Confederacy and establish trade relationships, driven by the South's production of cotton and other agricultural goods. The geopolitical dynamics of the 19th century are altered, with North America divided and potentially competing for influence and alliances.

## Modern America as Two Nations

### Social and Cultural Differences

In this alternate history, the two Americas develop distinct social and cultural identities. The Confederate States, rooted in traditional agrarian values and racial segregation, face ongoing social tensions and struggles for civil rights. The United States, influenced by the abolitionist movement and industrialization, becomes a more progressive society advocating for equality and social justice.

The cultural divergence between the North and South shapes art, literature, and education. Southern culture, with its emphasis on heritage and tradition, contrasts sharply with the North's focus on innovation, science, and cultural diversity. The two nations develop their own educational systems, media, and cultural institutions, reflecting their differing values and histories.

### Economic Development and Technological Progress

The economic development of the two nations follows divergent paths. The Confederate States, reliant on agriculture, face challenges in modernizing their economy. The lack of industrial infrastructure and innovation slows economic growth, leading to a reliance on foreign trade and investment. The United States, with its industrial base, advances rapidly, becoming a global leader in technology and innovation.

Technological progress in the North drives advancements in transportation, communication, and manufacturing. The development of railroads, telegraph systems, and mechanized industries transforms the economy and society. The South, slower to industrialize, struggles to keep pace with these changes, leading to economic disparities and social tensions.

Civil Rights and Social Justice

The legacy of slavery and racial segregation continues to haunt the Confederate States. The struggle for civil rights and equality becomes a central issue, with movements for emancipation and social justice facing significant opposition. The Confederate government, resistant to change, implements policies to maintain the status quo, leading to prolonged social conflict.

In the United States, the abolition of slavery and the push for civil rights drive significant social reforms. The Reconstruction era brings about changes in political representation, education, and labor rights. The North's commitment to social justice influences global movements for human rights and equality, positioning it as a leader in progressive social policies.

Long-Term Implications for Global History

Impact on World Wars

The divided Americas have significant implications for global conflicts, particularly the World Wars. The United States, with its industrial and military strength, plays a crucial role in both World War I and World War II. The Confederate States, with its weaker economy and military, may play a less significant role or align differently in these conflicts.

The presence of two distinct American nations affects global alliances and strategies. The United States' participation in the World Wars is driven by its industrial capacity and commitment to democratic principles. The Confederacy, with its focus on states' rights and limited central authority, may adopt a more isolationist stance or form different alliances, influencing the outcomes of global conflicts.

Influence on Decolonization and Civil Rights Movements

The divided Americas also impact global movements for decolonization and civil rights. The United States, as a champion of democracy and human rights, influences the decolonization efforts in Africa, Asia, and Latin America. The Confederate States, grappling with its own issues of racial inequality, has a more limited influence on these global movements.

The success of the civil rights movement in the United States inspires similar struggles worldwide. Leaders and activists draw inspiration from the American example, advocating for equality, justice, and human rights. The Confederate States' resistance to these movements highlights the global struggle for civil rights and the enduring impact of slavery and segregation.

Two Nations, Two Futures

In this alternate history, the victory of the South in the American Civil War creates a world characterized by division and disparity. The establishment of the Confederate States of America and the continued existence of the United States of America lead to distinct social, economic, and political paths. The legacy of slavery and racial inequality shapes the Confederate States, while the United States evolves as a progressive and industrialized nation.

By imagining a world where the South won the Civil War, we gain insights into the potential consequences of division and conflict. This alternate history highlights the importance of unity, equality, and social justice in shaping a prosperous and harmonious society. It reminds us that the choices and outcomes of pivotal moments in history have far-reaching implications for our shared future.

# Chapter 9: What If the Titanic Hadn't Sunk?

The Ill-Fated Voyage

The RMS Titanic, deemed "unsinkable," embarked on its maiden voyage from Southampton to New York City on April 10, 1912. This grand ship, the largest of its time, symbolized human ingenuity and luxury. Carrying over 2,200 passengers and crew, the Titanic was a marvel of modern engineering and opulence, with first-class accommodations that set new standards for maritime travel.

Tragically, on the night of April 14, 1912, the Titanic struck an iceberg in the North Atlantic and sank within a few hours. Over 1,500 people lost their lives in one of the deadliest maritime disasters in history. The sinking of the Titanic had profound effects on maritime safety regulations, leading to significant changes in the shipping industry to prevent such a tragedy from happening again.

Causes of the Disaster

The sinking of the Titanic was the result of a combination of factors, including the ship's design, the crew's actions, and environmental conditions. The ship's watertight compartments were not fully sealed, and the bulkheads did not extend high enough to prevent water from flooding multiple compartments. The lookout's delayed sighting of the iceberg and the ship's high speed in iceberg-prone waters also contributed to the disaster.

Additionally, the insufficient number of lifeboats on board was a critical issue. Although the Titanic carried more lifeboats than legally required at the time, there were not enough for all passengers and crew. The chaotic evacuation and lack of proper lifeboat drills further exacerbated the situation, leading to a high number of casualties.

A Safe Arrival

But what if the Titanic had not struck the iceberg and had safely completed its maiden voyage? How would this alternate history have impacted the passengers, the shipping industry, and the world at large?

Changes in Maritime Safety

In this alternate timeline, the Titanic successfully navigates the iceberg-laden waters and arrives safely in New York City. The ship's successful voyage solidifies its reputation as an engineering marvel, reinforcing the belief in its "unsinkable" nature. However, the absence of a major disaster delays the implementation of crucial maritime safety regulations.

Without the Titanic tragedy as a catalyst, the shipping industry continues operating under existing safety standards. The need for more lifeboats, better emergency procedures, and improved communication systems is not immediately recognized. It takes other maritime incidents and growing public concern to eventually prompt changes in safety regulations, but these reforms come more slowly and incrementally.

Impact on Passengers' Lives

The safe arrival of the Titanic profoundly affects the lives of its passengers and crew. Many prominent figures aboard the ship, such as industrialist John Jacob Astor IV, socialite Margaret "Molly" Brown, and businessman Benjamin Guggenheim, continue their influential roles in society. Their survival and ongoing contributions to various fields shape the course of history in unique ways.

For the hundreds of immigrant passengers in third class, the safe voyage offers new opportunities in America. These individuals and families go on to build new lives, contributing to the cultural and economic fabric of the United States. The survival of these passengers and crew members leads to countless personal stories of success, struggle, and legacy.

The Titanic's Legacy Today

Technological and Industrial Advancements

The successful completion of the Titanic's maiden voyage reinforces public confidence in the technological advancements of the early 20th century. The ship's engineering feats inspire further innovations in shipbuilding and maritime travel. Other shipping companies strive to match or surpass the Titanic's standards of luxury and safety, driving competition and technological progress.

The Titanic's legacy as a symbol of human ingenuity and ambition encourages continued investment in large-scale engineering projects. The lessons learned from the ship's construction and operation influence the design and development of future ocean liners, contributing to advancements in materials, construction techniques, and safety features.

Cultural and Social Impact

The safe arrival of the Titanic has a significant cultural and social impact. The ship's story becomes one of triumph and innovation rather than tragedy. It serves as a symbol of human achievement and the potential of modern technology. The Titanic's legacy is celebrated through literature, art, and media, inspiring works that highlight the ship's grandeur and the spirit of its time.

Museums and exhibitions dedicated to the Titanic's successful voyage attract visitors from around the world, preserving and showcasing artifacts and stories from the ship. The Titanic becomes a symbol of the early 20th century's optimism and progress, influencing popular culture and historical narratives.

Maritime Safety Reforms

Although the absence of the Titanic disaster delays immediate reforms, the shipping industry eventually recognizes the need for improved safety measures. Other maritime incidents and growing public awareness drive the adoption of stricter regulations. The establishment of international standards for lifeboats, emergency procedures, and communication systems enhances maritime safety over time.

The incremental reforms inspired by other incidents lead to a safer and more reliable shipping industry. The lessons learned from the Titanic's operation and subsequent maritime history contribute to the development of robust safety protocols, ensuring the well-being of passengers and crew on future voyages.

A Legacy of Triumph

In this alternate history, the successful completion of the Titanic's maiden voyage transforms its legacy from one of tragedy to triumph. The ship's safe arrival reinforces confidence in technological progress and human ingenuity, inspiring further advancements in maritime travel and engineering. The lives of the passengers and crew, spared from disaster, continue to shape the course of history in meaningful ways.

By imagining a world where the Titanic did not sink, we gain insights into the potential impact of pivotal events on technological innovation, cultural narratives, and personal histories. This alternate history reminds us of the importance of safety, preparedness, and the enduring influence of human ambition and resilience.

# Chapter 10: What If World War I Had Never Happened?

The Causes of World War I

World War I, also known as the Great War, erupted in 1914 and involved many of the world's major powers. The war's origins lay in a complex web of alliances, militarism, imperialism, and nationalism. Key events leading to the conflict included the assassination of Archduke Franz Ferdinand of Austria-Hungary, which acted as the immediate catalyst, and the subsequent mobilization of allied forces across Europe.

The intricate alliances between countries meant that a conflict involving one power quickly escalated into a full-scale war. The Central Powers, led by Germany, Austria-Hungary, and the Ottoman Empire, faced off against the Allied Powers, including France, Russia, and the United Kingdom. The war was characterized by trench warfare, massive casualties, and a significant impact on the political and social structures of the involved nations.

The Devastation of War

World War I caused unprecedented devastation. Over 16 million people, including soldiers and civilians, lost their lives. The war led to the collapse of empires, such as the Austro-Hungarian, Ottoman, Russian, and German empires, and significantly altered the political landscape of Europe. The Treaty of Versailles, which officially ended the war in 1919, imposed harsh penalties on Germany, contributing to economic hardship and political instability.

The war also had profound social and economic impacts. The mass mobilization of soldiers and resources disrupted economies and societies. The psychological trauma experienced by soldiers and civilians, known as "shell shock," highlighted the war's brutal nature. Technological advancements in weaponry, such as machine guns, tanks, and chemical warfare, further exemplified the war's destructive power.

A Peaceful 20th Century

But what if World War I had never happened? How would the absence of this global conflict have shaped the 20th century and beyond?

Technological and Social Developments

In this alternate timeline, the world avoids the catastrophic impact of World War I. Without the war, technological advancements continue to progress, but at a potentially slower and more measured pace. Innovations in fields such as aviation, medicine, and communication still occur, driven by peacetime research and development rather than wartime necessity.

The social fabric of nations remains intact, with fewer disruptions to family structures and economic stability. The absence of war-related trauma means a healthier and more stable population. Women's roles in society continue to evolve, but without the wartime push for labor, the progress is more gradual and less abrupt.

Political Landscape Without War

The political landscape of Europe and the world is significantly different without World War I. The Austro-Hungarian and Ottoman empires, while still facing internal pressures, avoid sudden collapse. This gradual change allows for more stable transitions of power and potentially fewer conflicts in the Middle East and Eastern Europe.

Germany, without the burden of the Treaty of Versailles, avoids the economic hardships and political instability that contributed to the rise of Adolf Hitler and the Nazi Party. The absence of World War I means no World War II, leading to a vastly different geopolitical environment in the mid-20th century. The political ideologies of fascism and communism may still emerge, but their influence and spread are likely different.

The World Today Without World War Istill competitive, avoid the crippling debt and reconstruction costs associated with post-war recovery.

The absence of the Great Depression, partly influenced by the economic instability following World War I, leads to sustained economic growth and prosperity in the 1920s and beyond. This stability fosters global trade and investment, leading to a more interconnected and prosperous world economy.

Cultural and Artistic Movements

The cultural and artistic movements of the 20th century take different forms without the influence of World War I. The trauma and disillusionment that fueled movements such as Dadaism and Surrealism are less pronounced, leading to different expressions of modernism in art and literature. The Jazz Age and the Roaring Twenties still occur, but with a greater sense of optimism and continuity.

The flourishing of arts and culture in this peaceful 20th century leads to new forms of creativity and innovation. The lack of a global conflict allows for uninterrupted cultural exchanges and collaborations, enriching the global cultural landscape. Literary and artistic works reflect the stability and progress of society, focusing on themes of innovation, exploration, and human potential.

Social and Political Reforms

The absence of World War I allows for more gradual and stable social and political reforms. Movements for women's suffrage, labor rights, and social justice continue to advance, but without the abrupt changes caused by wartime mobilization. The gradual integration of women into the workforce and political life leads to more sustained and systemic changes in gender equality.

Political reforms in Europe and the Americas continue to evolve, driven by democratic ideals and economic stability. The avoidance of extremist ideologies and totalitarian regimes creates a political environment conducive to cooperation and progress. International organizations, such as the League of Nations or a similar body, emerge to promote global peace and cooperation.

Impact on Global Conflicts and Cooperation (1,500 words)

Avoidance of World War II

The absence of World War I and the resulting political stability prevent the conditions that led to World War II. The lack of the Treaty of Versailles means Germany does not face the same economic and political pressures that fueled the rise of Hitler and the Nazi Party. European powers focus on diplomacy and cooperation rather than conflict and retribution.

Without World War II, the Holocaust and other atrocities are avoided, preserving millions of lives and preventing immense suffering. The global focus on peace and stability leads to the establishment of international norms and institutions aimed at preventing future conflicts and promoting human rights.

Influence on Decolonization and Global Relations

The absence of the World Wars influences the pace and nature of decolonization. European powers, without the economic and political strain of global conflicts, approach decolonization more gradually and cooperatively. The transition of colonies to independent nations is less violent and more stable, leading to better outcomes for newly independent states.

Global relations are characterized by increased cooperation and diplomacy. The establishment of international organizations promotes dialogue and conflict resolution. The focus on economic development and social progress fosters a more interconnected and cooperative world, reducing the likelihood of large-scale conflicts.

A Century of Peace and Progress

In this alternate history, the absence of World War I creates a world characterized by peace, stability, and progress. The technological, social, and political developments of the 20th century occur in a more stable and gradual manner, leading to sustained economic growth and cultural flourishing. The avoidance of global conflicts and the focus on cooperation and diplomacy shape a more interconnected and prosperous world.

By imagining a world without World War I, we gain insights into the potential for human progress when not hindered by devastating conflicts. This alternate history reminds us of the importance of peace, cooperation, and the enduring impact of pivotal moments in history on our shared future.

# Chapter 11: What If the Stock Market Crash of 1929 Had Been Averted?

The Roaring Twenties

The 1920s, often referred to as the "Roaring Twenties," was a decade of economic prosperity and cultural dynamism in the United States and much of the Western world. Following the end of World War I, there was a significant shift towards consumerism, with rapid advancements in technology, transportation, and entertainment. The widespread adoption of automobiles, radios, and household appliances transformed daily life, while jazz music, flapper fashion, and the Harlem Renaissance defined the era's cultural landscape.

Economic growth during the 1920s was fueled by industrial expansion, technological innovation, and speculative investments in the stock market. The stock market boom led many Americans to invest heavily, often on margin, creating an unsustainable bubble. The decade's exuberance, however, masked underlying economic weaknesses, such as income inequality, overproduction, and agricultural distress.

Causes of the Great Depression

The stock market crash of October 1929 marked the beginning of the Great Depression, a severe worldwide economic downturn that lasted throughout the 1930s. Several factors contributed to the crash and the ensuing economic collapse:

Speculative Investments: Many investors bought stocks on margin, borrowing money to purchase shares, which inflated stock prices to unsustainable levels.

Bank Failures: The banking system was fragile, with many banks overexposed to the stock market. When the market crashed, banks failed, leading to a loss of savings and a contraction of credit.

Agricultural Problems: Farmers faced falling crop prices and mounting debts, exacerbating rural poverty and economic instability.

Global Trade Decline: Tariffs and trade barriers, such as the Smoot-Hawley Tariff, reduced international trade, worsening the global economic situation.

The Great Depression led to widespread unemployment, poverty, and social upheaval. It prompted significant changes in economic policy and governance, including the New Deal in the United States, which aimed to provide relief, recovery, and reform to the struggling nation.

Averted Stock Market Crash

But what if the stock market crash of 1929 had been averted? How would this alternate history have shaped the economic and social development of the United States and the world?

Preventative Measures and Economic Stability

In this alternate timeline, key financial and regulatory measures are implemented in the mid-1920s to curb speculative investments and stabilize the economy. These measures include stricter regulations on margin lending, improved banking oversight, and policies to address agricultural distress and income inequality.

The Federal Reserve, recognizing the signs of an overheated market, takes proactive steps to manage interest rates and credit availability. By cooling the speculative fervor and ensuring a more stable banking system, the stock market avoids the dramatic crash of October 1929. As a result, the economy experiences a more gradual correction rather than a severe collapse.

Sustained Economic Growth

With the stock market crash averted, the United States avoids the immediate onset of the Great Depression. Economic growth, though moderated, continues through the late 1920s and into the 1930s. The increased stability fosters investment in infrastructure, technology, and industry, leading to sustained economic expansion.

The absence of a severe economic downturn allows for continued consumer confidence and spending. The growth of the middle class and the expansion of consumer markets drive demand for goods and services, further fueling economic growth. The improved economic conditions also support better wages and working conditions, contributing to a more prosperous and equitable society.

Impact on Global Markets

International Economic Stability

The averted crash and continued economic growth in the United States have significant positive effects on global markets. The stability of the American economy supports international trade and investment, fostering economic growth in other countries. The global financial system remains more robust, avoiding the widespread bank failures and credit contractions that characterized the Great Depression.

European economies, recovering from the impacts of World War I, benefit from continued trade with the United States. The absence of the Great Depression allows for more stable political and economic conditions in Europe, reducing the appeal of extremist ideologies and potentially altering the course of events leading to World War II.

Technological and Industrial Advancements

The sustained economic growth of the 1930s drives technological and industrial advancements. Investment in research and development leads to significant breakthroughs in various fields, including transportation, communication, and medicine. The continued expansion of industries such as automotive, aviation, and electronics transforms daily life and creates new economic opportunities.

The improved economic conditions also support the growth of the entertainment and media industries. The rise of Hollywood, the proliferation of radio, and the early development of television shape cultural trends and influence global culture. The technological advancements and cultural innovations of this period set the stage for the rapid development of the mid-20th century.

Social and Political Reforms

The absence of the Great Depression influences the trajectory of social and political reforms. The New Deal, with its extensive government intervention in the economy, is not implemented. Instead, gradual and incremental reforms address social and economic issues. Labor rights, social welfare programs, and regulatory frameworks evolve more steadily, driven by public demand and political negotiation.

The continued economic stability fosters a political environment focused on collaboration and progress. The establishment of social safety nets, improved labor conditions, and investment in public infrastructure contribute to a more equitable and inclusive society. The absence of extreme economic hardship reduces social unrest and political polarization, promoting a more cooperative and democratic political landscape.

The World Today Without the Great Depression

Economic Landscape

The world today, in this alternate history, is characterized by sustained economic growth and stability. The United States, avoiding the severe economic downturn of the Great Depression, maintains its position as a global economic leader. The continued investment in technology and infrastructure drives innovation and productivity, leading to a higher standard of living.

The global economy benefits from the stability and growth of the American economy. International trade and investment flourish, fostering economic development in various regions. The absence of the Great Depression and the subsequent economic recovery efforts create a more resilient and interconnected global economy.

Social Progress and Equality

The sustained economic growth supports ongoing social progress and equality. The expansion of educational opportunities, healthcare, and social welfare programs improves quality of life and reduces poverty. The gradual integration of women and minorities into the workforce and political life fosters a more inclusive and equitable society.

The cultural and social developments of the 20th century reflect the optimism and progress of a world without the Great Depression. The civil rights movement, women's liberation, and other social justice initiatives continue to advance, driven by the stability and prosperity of the post-1920s period. The absence of severe economic hardship allows for a more focused and sustained push for equality and justice.

Global Influence and Leadership

The United States, maintaining its economic and political stability, plays a leading role in global affairs. The absence of the Great Depression and the New Deal leads to a different approach to international relations and economic policy. The focus on diplomacy, trade, and cooperation shapes a more peaceful and prosperous global order.

The sustained economic growth and stability of the United States influence global political dynamics, promoting democratic governance and economic development. The absence of extreme economic conditions reduces the appeal of totalitarian regimes, fostering a more stable and cooperative international environment.

A World of Prosperity and Progress

In this alternate history, the averted stock market crash of 1929 creates a world characterized by sustained economic growth, stability, and progress. The absence of the Great Depression allows for continued investment in technology, infrastructure, and social welfare, leading to a higher standard of living and greater equality. The impact on global markets and international relations fosters a more interconnected and prosperous world.

By imagining a world without the stock market crash of 1929, we gain insights into the potential for human progress and the importance of economic stability. This alternate history reminds us of the interconnectedness of global economies and the enduring impact of pivotal moments on our shared future.

# Chapter 12: What If World War II Had Never Happened?

The Rise of Totalitarianism

The interwar period between World War I and World War II saw the rise of totalitarian regimes in Europe and Asia. In Germany, economic hardship and political instability facilitated the rise of Adolf Hitler and the Nazi Party. Hitler's aggressive expansionist policies and racist ideology led to the invasion of Poland in 1939, sparking World War II. Similarly, in Italy, Benito Mussolini established a fascist regime, while in Japan, militarists pursued aggressive expansion in East Asia.

These regimes sought to overturn the post-World War I international order, driven by ambitions of territorial expansion and domination. The failure of the League of Nations to prevent aggression and the policy of appeasement practiced by major powers like Britain and France only emboldened these dictatorships, setting the stage for global conflict.

Key Events Leading to War

Several key events and decisions contributed to the outbreak of World War II:

Treaty of Versailles: The harsh terms imposed on Germany after World War I fostered resentment and economic hardship, creating fertile ground for extremist ideologies.

Appeasement: The policy of appeasing Hitler's demands, such as the Munich Agreement in 1938, allowed Nazi Germany to grow stronger and more emboldened.

Invasion of Poland: Germany's invasion of Poland in September 1939, followed by Britain and France's declarations of war, marked the official start of World War II.

Japanese Expansion: Japan's invasion of Manchuria in 1931 and subsequent aggression in China and the Pacific aimed to establish Japanese dominance in Asia.

These events led to a conflict that engulfed much of the world, resulting in unprecedented devastation and loss of life.

A World Without World War II

But what if World War II had never happened? How would the absence of this global conflict have shaped the mid-20th century and beyond?

Political Landscape and International Relations

In this alternate timeline, key events and decisions prevent the outbreak of World War II. The Treaty of Versailles is more lenient, promoting economic recovery and political stability in Germany. The rise of extremist regimes is countered by effective international cooperation and intervention. The League of Nations, strengthened by reforms, successfully mediates conflicts and enforces peace agreements.

Without World War II, the political landscape of Europe and Asia remains more stable. Democracies and moderate governments retain power, preventing the spread of totalitarian ideologies. International relations are characterized by diplomacy and cooperation, fostering a more peaceful and interconnected world.

Technological and Social Progress

The absence of World War II significantly impacts technological and social progress. While wartime research and development contributed to major technological advancements, these innovations still occur in a peacetime context, driven by scientific curiosity and economic competition.

Technological progress in fields such as aviation, medicine, and nuclear energy continues, but with a focus on civilian applications. The absence of the war's destructive impact allows for more sustained investment in education, healthcare, and infrastructure, leading to a higher quality of life and greater social progress.

Changes in Global Alliances

United States and Soviet Union

The absence of World War II significantly alters the relationship between the United States and the Soviet Union. Without the wartime alliance and subsequent Cold War, the ideological divide between capitalism and communism is less pronounced. The United States focuses on domestic growth and international trade, while the Soviet Union, under more moderate leadership, pursues economic and social reforms.

The lack of a Cold War leads to different global alliances and geopolitical dynamics. International organizations, such as a reformed League of Nations, play a more significant role in mediating conflicts and promoting cooperation. The absence of a nuclear arms race reduces global tensions and fosters a more stable international environment.

Europe and Asia

In Europe, the absence of World War II allows for more gradual political and economic integration. The European powers focus on rebuilding and cooperation, leading to the early establishment of institutions that promote unity and economic collaboration. The formation of a European Union-like entity occurs sooner, fostering peace and prosperity on the continent.

In Asia, Japan's expansionist policies are curtailed by effective international intervention and diplomatic pressure. China, without the devastation of the Sino-Japanese War and subsequent conflict, experiences more stable development. The absence of Japanese occupation allows for stronger economic growth and political stability in the region.

Decolonization and Global Movements

The process of decolonization occurs more gradually and peacefully without the destabilizing impact of World War II. European powers, facing less economic strain, are better able to manage the transition of their colonies to independence. The formation of new nations is characterized by negotiated settlements and international support, leading to more stable and prosperous post-colonial states.

Global movements for civil rights, women's liberation, and social justice continue to advance, driven by the stability and progress of the mid-20th century. The absence of global conflict allows for a greater focus on social reforms and equality, leading to significant improvements in human rights and social conditions worldwide.

Impact on Culture and Society

Cultural Renaissance

The absence of World War II fosters a cultural renaissance, as resources and attention are devoted to the arts, education, and intellectual pursuits. The cultural movements of the 20th century, such as modernism and postmodernism, evolve in a context of stability and progress. The exchange of ideas and artistic collaboration flourishes, leading to innovative and influential works in literature, music, and visual arts.

The growth of media and communication technologies further enhances cultural exchange. The development of television, cinema, and radio creates new platforms for storytelling and artistic expression, shaping cultural trends and societal values.

Social Reforms and Equality

The sustained economic growth and stability of this alternate timeline support ongoing social reforms. Movements for civil rights and social justice gain momentum, leading to significant advances in equality and human rights. The absence of the Holocaust and other wartime atrocities prevents the deep scars of racial and ethnic hatred, fostering a more inclusive and tolerant society.

The push for gender equality continues, driven by the integration of women into the workforce and political life. Education and social policies promote equal opportunities, leading to greater representation and empowerment of women and minorities in all aspects of society.

The Modern World Without World War II

Economic and Technological Landscape

In this alternate history, the world enjoys sustained economic growth and technological progress. The global economy is characterized by stability and cooperation, with international trade and investment driving prosperity. Technological advancements continue to transform daily life, improving healthcare, transportation, and communication.

The absence of war-related destruction allows for uninterrupted development and innovation. The focus on sustainable growth and environmental stewardship leads to a more balanced and equitable global economy. Advances in science and technology are driven by peaceful competition and collaboration, fostering a brighter and more prosperous future.

Political Stability and Global Governance

The political stability of this alternate timeline supports the development of effective global governance structures. International organizations, such as a reformed League of Nations or a precursor to the United Nations, play a central role in maintaining peace and promoting cooperation. The focus on diplomacy and conflict resolution prevents large-scale wars and fosters a culture of collaboration.

The success of these international efforts influences the development of global norms and standards, promoting democracy, human rights, and the rule of law. The absence of major global conflicts allows for the peaceful resolution of disputes and the advancement of collective security.

A World of Peace and Progress

In this alternate history, the absence of World War II creates a world characterized by peace, stability, and progress. The technological, social, and political developments of the mid-20th century occur in a more stable and gradual manner, leading to sustained economic growth and cultural flourishing. The impact on global alliances, decolonization, and social movements fosters a more interconnected and equitable world.

By imagining a world without World War II, we gain insights into the potential for human progress when not hindered by devastating conflicts. This alternate history reminds us of the importance of peace, cooperation, and the enduring impact of pivotal moments on our shared future.

# Chapter 13: What If the Space Race Had Continued?

The Early Space Race

The Space Race, a period of intense competition between the United States and the Soviet Union, began in the late 1950s and continued through the 1960s. It was marked by significant milestones, including the launch of Sputnik, the first artificial satellite, by the Soviet Union in 1957, and the subsequent achievements of the United States, culminating in the Apollo 11 moon landing in 1969.

This period of competition was driven by Cold War tensions, with both superpowers seeking to demonstrate technological and ideological superiority. The Space Race led to rapid advancements in rocket technology, space exploration, and scientific research, capturing the imagination of people around the world and inspiring a generation of scientists and engineers.

Achievements and Milestones

The Space Race saw numerous groundbreaking achievements:

Sputnik (1957): The Soviet Union launched Sputnik, the first artificial satellite, marking the beginning of space exploration.

Vostok 1 (1961): Yuri Gagarin became the first human to orbit the Earth, a major milestone for the Soviet space program.

Apollo 11 (1969): The United States successfully landed astronauts Neil Armstrong and Buzz Aldrin on the Moon, fulfilling President John F. Kennedy's goal and marking a significant victory for NASA.

These achievements showcased the potential of human space exploration and laid the foundation for future missions. However, by the early 1970s, the fervor of the Space Race had cooled, with both nations facing economic pressures and shifting priorities.

Continued Competition

But what if the Space Race had continued with the same intensity and competition? How would ongoing rivalry and investment in space exploration have shaped the late 20th and early 21st centuries?

Advancements in Space Technology

In this alternate timeline, the United States and the Soviet Union continue their intense competition in space exploration. The ongoing rivalry drives significant advancements in technology and innovation. Both nations invest heavily in developing new spacecraft, propulsion systems, and space habitats.

The focus shifts from achieving single milestones to establishing a sustained human presence in space. Both nations embark on ambitious missions to build space stations, lunar bases, and eventually, missions to Mars. The technological advancements made during this period lead to the development of reusable rockets, advanced life support systems, and efficient propulsion methods, significantly reducing the cost and increasing the feasibility of space travel.

Scientific Discoveries and Exploration

The continuation of the Space Race accelerates scientific discoveries and exploration. Robotic missions to the outer planets and their moons provide valuable data on the solar system, while telescopes and observatories in space enhance our understanding of the universe. The ongoing competition leads to joint missions and collaborative projects, fostering international cooperation in scientific research.

The establishment of lunar bases serves as a stepping stone for further exploration. Scientists conduct extensive research on the Moon's geology, resources, and potential for sustaining human life. The presence of astronauts on the Moon provides insights into long-duration space missions, informing future journeys to Mars and beyond.

Colonization of Space

Lunar Bases and Settlements

In this alternate history, both the United States and the Soviet Union establish permanent bases on the Moon by the late 1980s. These bases serve as hubs for scientific research, resource extraction, and technological development. The lessons learned from maintaining these lunar outposts pave the way for more ambitious space colonization efforts.

Lunar settlements grow over time, supported by advancements in life support systems, energy production, and sustainable living practices. The extraction of resources such as water ice and minerals supports the development of infrastructure and the production of rocket fuel, reducing the reliance on Earth-based supplies.

Mars Missions and Colonization

Building on the success of lunar bases, both nations set their sights on Mars. By the early 2000s, manned missions to Mars become a reality. These missions focus on exploring the Martian surface, searching for signs of past or present life, and assessing the planet's potential for human colonization.

The establishment of Martian colonies follows, with habitats designed to withstand the harsh environment and support long-term human habitation. Advances in biotechnology, robotics, and artificial intelligence play a crucial role in ensuring the success and sustainability of these colonies. The competition between the United States and the

Soviet Union drives continuous improvements in technology and infrastructure, making Mars a second home for humanity.

The Modern Era of Space Exploration

International Collaboration and Commercial Spaceflight

As the Space Race continues, the focus shifts from rivalry to collaboration. Recognizing the benefits of pooling resources and expertise, the United States and the Soviet Union, along with other emerging spacefaring nations, form international partnerships. These collaborations lead to the creation of multinational space agencies and joint missions, fostering a spirit of cooperation and shared goals.

The commercialization of space also accelerates. Private companies, inspired by government-led successes and supported by favorable policies, enter the space industry. Innovations from the private sector, such as reusable rockets and space tourism, expand access to space and reduce costs. The commercial space industry thrives, driving further advancements and opening new opportunities for exploration and exploitation of space resources.

Technological and Social Impact

The ongoing investment in space exploration and technology has profound impacts on society. Innovations developed for space missions find applications on Earth, leading to advancements in healthcare, environmental monitoring, energy production, and materials science. The technology transfer from space programs drives economic growth and improves quality of life.

The cultural impact of continued space exploration is significant. The presence of humans on the Moon and Mars captures the public's imagination and inspires a new generation of scientists, engineers, and explorers. Space exploration becomes a symbol of human ingenuity and the pursuit of knowledge, fostering a sense of global unity and purpose.

The Future of Space Exploration

Beyond Mars: Asteroid Mining and Deep Space Missions

With the success of lunar and Martian colonies, the focus of space exploration shifts to more distant targets. Asteroid mining becomes a major industry, providing valuable resources such as rare metals and water. These resources support further space exploration and the development of infrastructure in space.

Deep space missions, including manned missions to the outer planets and their moons, become feasible with advancements in propulsion technology and life support systems. The exploration of Europa, Titan, and other celestial bodies provides new insights into the potential for life beyond Earth and expands our understanding of the solar system.

The Search for Extraterrestrial Life

The continued exploration of space fuels the search for extraterrestrial life. Missions to Mars, Europa, and other potentially habitable environments focus on detecting signs of life and understanding the conditions that support it. The discovery of microbial life on another planet would have profound implications for science, philosophy, and our understanding of our place in the universe.

The development of advanced telescopes and observatories allows for the study of exoplanets in greater detail. The search for Earth-like planets in the habitable zones of distant stars becomes a major scientific endeavor, driving the quest to answer one of humanity's oldest questions: Are we alone in the universe?

A Bold Future in Space

In this alternate history, the continuation of the Space Race leads to remarkable advancements in space exploration and technology. The intense competition between the United States and the Soviet Union drives humanity to establish a sustained presence on the Moon and Mars, fostering international collaboration and commercial innovation.

The impact of continued space exploration extends beyond the scientific and technological realms. It inspires a sense of global unity and purpose, challenging humanity to push the boundaries of what is possible. The pursuit of knowledge and the quest to explore the cosmos become defining aspects of our shared future, shaping a world that values innovation, cooperation, and the endless possibilities of the universe.

By imagining a world where the Space Race never ended, we gain insights into the potential for human achievement and the importance of exploration in driving progress. This alternate history reminds us that the spirit of discovery and the pursuit of knowledge are fundamental to our identity as a species, guiding us toward a bold and exciting future in space.

# Chapter 14: What If the Internet Had Never Been Invented?

The Birth of the Internet

The Internet, as we know it today, began as a project in the 1960s under the U.S. Department of Defense's Advanced Research Projects Agency (ARPA). Known as ARPANET, this early network was designed to facilitate communication between research institutions and military establishments. The development of key technologies such as packet switching and the TCP/IP protocol laid the foundation for the modern Internet.

Throughout the 1980s and 1990s, the Internet evolved rapidly. The introduction of the World Wide Web by Tim Berners-Lee in 1989 revolutionized the way information was shared and accessed. By the mid-1990s, the Internet had become a global phenomenon, transforming communication, commerce, education, and entertainment. Today, the Internet is an integral part of daily life, connecting billions of people and enabling countless innovations.

Early Influences and Development

The development of the Internet was influenced by various technological and social factors:

Computing Advances: The invention of the computer and subsequent advances in computing technology were critical to the development of the Internet.

Communication Needs: The need for efficient and reliable communication networks, especially during the Cold War, drove the development of early networking technologies.

Research Collaboration: The desire for collaboration among researchers and academics spurred the creation of networks that could share information quickly and effectively.

These factors, combined with the ingenuity and vision of early pioneers, led to the creation of a global network that transformed society in profound ways.

A World Without the Internet

But what if the Internet had never been invented? How would the absence of this transformative technology have shaped the late 20th and early 21st centuries?

Communication and Information Sharing

In this alternate timeline, the lack of the Internet fundamentally alters the way people communicate and share information. Traditional forms of communication, such as telephone, mail, and fax, remain dominant. While these methods are effective, they lack the speed and convenience of digital communication.

The dissemination of information is slower and more limited. Libraries, physical media, and broadcast television and radio continue to be the primary sources of information. The absence of instant access to vast amounts of information impacts education, research, and news dissemination, making these processes more time-consuming and less efficient.

Technological and Social Impact

The absence of the Internet slows the pace of technological innovation and social change. Many of the advancements in fields such as e-commerce, social media, and cloud computing are never realized. The tech industry, as we know it, develops differently, with a focus on hardware and software for standalone systems rather than interconnected networks.

Socially, the lack of the Internet means that people rely more on face-to-face interactions and traditional forms of socializing. While this fosters strong local communities, it limits the ability to connect with people across the globe. The spread of ideas and cultural exchange is slower and less widespread, impacting globalization and the development of a global culture.

Communication and Information Sharing

Traditional Media and Publishing

Without the Internet, traditional media such as newspapers, magazines, and books remain the primary sources of information and entertainment. The publishing industry continues to thrive, with print media playing a central role in disseminating news and knowledge. Television and radio also remain vital for real-time information and entertainment.

The absence of digital platforms means that news is less immediate and more curated. Journalists and editors play a significant role in shaping public discourse, and the speed of news dissemination is constrained by the limitations of print and broadcast media. While this may lead to more thoughtful and well-researched journalism, it also means that breaking news and real-time updates are less accessible.

Communication Technologies

The evolution of communication technologies follows a different path without the Internet. The development of advanced telecommunication systems, such as satellite and fiber optic networks, continues to improve long-distance communication. However, these systems are used primarily for voice and limited data transmission rather than the vast data exchange enabled by the Internet.

Social interactions rely heavily on traditional methods such as telephone calls, letters, and in-person meetings. While these methods foster strong personal connections, they lack the convenience and immediacy of digital communication. The development of mobile communication devices, such as smartphones, is also impacted, as these devices are designed primarily for voice communication and limited text messaging.

Technological and Economic Development

Industry and Innovation

The absence of the Internet impacts various industries and the pace of innovation. The tech industry, in particular, develops differently, focusing on hardware and software for standalone systems rather than interconnected networks. Innovations in fields such as e-commerce, cloud computing, and digital services are significantly delayed or never realized.

Other industries, such as finance, healthcare, and education, also experience slower technological advancement. The lack of digital platforms for online banking, telemedicine, and e-learning means that these services remain more traditional and less accessible. The pace of automation and efficiency improvements in these sectors is slower, impacting overall economic growth and productivity.

Globalization and Trade

Globalization progresses at a slower pace without the Internet. International trade and commerce rely more on traditional methods of communication and transportation, limiting the speed and efficiency of global supply chains. The exchange of goods and services is less streamlined, impacting global economic integration and growth.

The development of global markets and international business is also affected. Multinational corporations face greater challenges in managing global operations and coordinating across different regions. The absence of digital communication tools and platforms means that international collaboration and cooperation are more difficult and time-consuming.

Social and Cultural Impact

Social Interaction and Community

The absence of the Internet profoundly affects social interaction and community building. People rely more on face-to-face interactions and traditional forms of socializing, such as community events, clubs, and local organizations. While this fosters strong local communities and personal connections, it limits the ability to connect with people across the globe.

The spread of ideas and cultural exchange is slower and more localized. The development of global communities and networks, such as social media platforms and online forums, is significantly impacted. Cultural trends and movements spread more gradually, and the creation of global cultural phenomena is less common.

Education and Research

Education and research are also significantly impacted by the absence of the Internet. Traditional methods of learning, such as textbooks, lectures, and physical libraries, remain the primary sources of knowledge. The accessibility of information is limited, and the ability to conduct research and access academic resources is more constrained.

The development of online learning platforms and digital educational resources is delayed or never realized. This impacts the accessibility and flexibility of education, particularly for remote and underserved communities. The pace of scientific and academic collaboration is slower, as researchers rely on traditional methods of communication and information sharing.

The Modern Digital Landscape

Technological Innovation and Development

In this alternate history, technological innovation and development follow a different trajectory. While advancements in computing, telecommunications, and electronics continue, the absence of the

Internet means that these innovations are applied in different ways. The focus is on standalone systems and specialized applications rather than interconnected networks and digital ecosystems.

The development of technologies such as artificial intelligence, big data, and the Internet of Things is significantly impacted. These technologies rely on the connectivity and data exchange enabled by the Internet, and their growth is limited in its absence. The potential for smart cities, connected devices, and automated systems is constrained, impacting the overall pace of technological progress.

Social and Economic Impact

The social and economic impact of the absence of the Internet is profound. While traditional industries and methods of communication continue to thrive, the potential for digital transformation and innovation is limited. This impacts overall economic growth and productivity, as well as the ability to address global challenges such as climate change, healthcare, and education.

The absence of the Internet also impacts social dynamics and the way people interact with each other. The reliance on traditional methods of communication and socializing fosters strong personal connections but limits the ability to connect with people across the globe. The spread of ideas and cultural exchange is slower, impacting the development of a global culture and community.

A World Without the Internet

In this alternate history, the absence of the Internet creates a world that is more reliant on traditional methods of communication, information sharing, and technological innovation. While this fosters strong local communities and personal connections, it limits the potential for global connectivity and digital transformation.

The impact of the Internet on our daily lives, industries, and society is profound, and imagining a world without it highlights the importance of connectivity and information sharing in driving progress and innovation. This alternate history reminds us of the transformative power of technology and the potential for human achievement when we embrace new ideas and possibilities.

By exploring a world without the Internet, we gain insights into the potential challenges and opportunities of technological innovation and the importance of fostering a connected and informed global community. This alternate history encourages us to reflect on the impact of the Internet on our lives and to continue exploring new ways to harness its potential for the betterment of humanity.

# Chapter 15: What If Climate Change Had Been Addressed Earlier?

Early Signs of Climate Change

The scientific community began recognizing the potential impacts of climate change as early as the mid-20th century. In the 1950s, scientists such as Charles David Keeling started measuring atmospheric carbon dioxide levels, which showed a clear upward trend. By the 1970s and 1980s, the evidence linking human activities, particularly the burning of fossil fuels, to global warming became more compelling.

Reports like the 1979 Charney Report and the 1988 establishment of the Intergovernmental Panel on Climate Change (IPCC) highlighted the risks of increasing greenhouse gas emissions. Despite these warnings, global action to address climate change was slow, hindered by political, economic, and social challenges.

Missed Opportunities

Throughout the latter half of the 20th century, several opportunities to address climate change were missed. Key international conferences, such as the 1992 Earth Summit in Rio de Janeiro and the 1997 Kyoto

Protocol, aimed to curb emissions but faced significant obstacles. The reluctance of major emitters, economic concerns, and political opposition slowed progress.

Industries reliant on fossil fuels resisted changes that could impact their profitability. Additionally, the complexity of global climate policies and the need for widespread cooperation made it difficult to implement effective solutions. As a result, global greenhouse gas emissions continued to rise, leading to more severe and widespread impacts of climate change.

A Proactive Approach

But what if the world had taken a proactive approach to address climate change earlier? How would the early recognition and action on climate change have shaped our environment, economy, and society?

Environmental Policies and Innovations

In this alternate timeline, the scientific consensus on climate change gains widespread acceptance in the 1970s and 1980s. Governments, recognizing the urgency of the issue, implement comprehensive environmental policies aimed at reducing greenhouse gas emissions. These policies include:

Carbon Pricing: Governments introduce carbon taxes and cap-and-trade systems to incentivize reductions in emissions and promote clean energy solutions.

Renewable Energy Investments: Significant investments are made in renewable energy sources such as solar, wind, and hydroelectric power, reducing reliance on fossil fuels.

Energy Efficiency Standards: Stricter energy efficiency standards are implemented for buildings, vehicles, and appliances, leading to substantial reductions in energy consumption.

Reforestation and Conservation: Large-scale reforestation projects and conservation efforts are launched to sequester carbon and preserve biodiversity.

These early actions drive innovation and technological advancements in the clean energy sector. The development and deployment of renewable energy technologies accelerate, leading to a significant reduction in greenhouse gas emissions.

Impact on Global Health and Economy

The proactive approach to climate change yields significant benefits for global health and the economy. The reduction in air pollution from decreased fossil fuel use leads to improved public health outcomes, with lower rates of respiratory and cardiovascular diseases. The shift to renewable energy creates new industries and job opportunities, driving economic growth and diversification.

The early adoption of sustainable practices and technologies also enhances energy security and reduces geopolitical tensions over fossil fuel resources. Countries invest in resilient infrastructure and sustainable agriculture, reducing the vulnerability to climate-related disasters and food insecurity.

The World Today with Early Action on Climate Change

Environmental and Ecological Impact

In this alternate history, the proactive approach to climate change results in a healthier and more resilient planet. The early reduction in greenhouse gas emissions slows the rate of global warming, mitigating many of the adverse effects associated with climate change. Key environmental impacts include:

Stabilized Climate: The global temperature rise is kept below critical thresholds, preventing the worst impacts of climate change, such as extreme weather events, sea-level rise, and ecosystem disruption.

Preserved Ecosystems: Biodiversity conservation efforts and reduced habitat destruction protect ecosystems and wildlife, maintaining ecological balance and resilience.

Reduced Ocean Acidification: The decrease in carbon dioxide emissions slows the acidification of oceans, preserving marine life and coral reefs.

The environmental benefits of early action on climate change enhance the planet's ability to support diverse life forms and provide essential ecosystem services.

Technological and Social Advancements

The proactive approach to climate change drives technological and social advancements. The early investment in clean energy technologies leads to significant breakthroughs, making renewable energy the dominant source of power. Innovations in energy storage, grid management, and sustainable transportation transform the way societies produce and consume energy.

Socially, the focus on sustainability and environmental stewardship fosters a culture of conservation and responsibility. Educational programs and public awareness campaigns promote sustainable lifestyles and environmental ethics. Communities and businesses prioritize sustainability in their practices, leading to widespread adoption of green technologies and behaviors.

Global Cooperation and Governance

The early recognition of climate change as a global challenge promotes international cooperation and effective governance. Countries collaborate on research, technology transfer, and policy implementation, sharing best practices and resources to address climate change. International organizations, such as a strengthened United Nations, play a crucial role in coordinating global efforts and ensuring compliance with climate agreements.

The success of early climate action sets a precedent for addressing other global challenges, such as poverty, inequality, and health. The collaborative approach to climate change fosters a sense of global solidarity and shared responsibility, enhancing international relations and promoting peace.

Long-Term Implications for the Future

Sustainable Development

The proactive approach to climate change lays the foundation for sustainable development. The integration of environmental considerations into economic and social planning ensures that development goals are achieved without compromising the planet's health. Key aspects of sustainable development include:

Circular Economy: The transition to a circular economy minimizes waste and maximizes resource efficiency, promoting recycling, reuse, and sustainable production practices.

Green Infrastructure: Investments in green infrastructure, such as urban green spaces, sustainable transportation systems, and resilient buildings, enhance the quality of life and reduce environmental impacts.

Equitable Growth: Sustainable development prioritizes social equity, ensuring that all communities benefit from economic growth and environmental protection.

The focus on sustainability drives innovation and entrepreneurship, creating new opportunities for economic development and improving overall well-being.

Resilience and Adaptation

The early action on climate change enhances the resilience of communities and ecosystems to climate-related impacts. Investments in resilient infrastructure, disaster preparedness, and adaptive capacity reduce vulnerability to extreme weather events and other climate risks. Key strategies for building resilience include:

Disaster Risk Reduction: Implementing early warning systems, emergency response plans, and community-based disaster preparedness programs minimizes the impact of natural disasters.

Adaptive Agriculture: Developing climate-resilient crops and sustainable agricultural practices ensures food security and supports rural livelihoods.

Water Management: Implementing integrated water management strategies ensures the sustainable use and conservation of water resources, reducing the risk of water scarcity and conflicts.

The proactive approach to climate change fosters a culture of resilience and preparedness, enhancing the ability of societies to adapt to changing conditions and thrive in the face of challenges.

A Healthier and More Sustainable World

In this alternate history, the early recognition and proactive action on climate change create a healthier, more resilient, and sustainable world. The environmental, technological, and social benefits of early climate action demonstrate the potential for human ingenuity and cooperation to address global challenges. By imagining a world where climate change was addressed earlier, we gain insights into the importance of timely and decisive action in shaping a sustainable future.

This alternate history reminds us that the choices we make today have profound implications for the future. It encourages us to embrace innovative solutions, foster international cooperation, and prioritize sustainability in all aspects of life. By learning from the past and taking proactive steps, we can create a better world for future generations, ensuring a healthy and thriving planet for all.

# Chapter 16: Conclusion

Reflections on Alternate Histories

Throughout this book, we've explored fifteen pivotal moments in history and imagined how different our world might be if events had unfolded differently. These alternate histories offer us a unique lens through which to view the past, highlighting the significance of individual decisions and actions in shaping the course of human events.

By delving into these "what if" scenarios, we gain a deeper appreciation for the complexity and interconnectedness of history. Each chapter has shown us that even small changes in historical events can have profound and far-reaching consequences. From the survival of dinosaurs to the avoidance of world wars, these alternate timelines remind us of the delicate balance that has brought us to our present reality.

The Power of Imagination

Imagining alternate histories is not just an exercise in creative thinking; it also helps us understand the importance of critical moments in our own lives. The power of imagination allows us to explore different possibilities and outcomes, encouraging us to think more deeply about the choices we make and their potential impact on the future.

As we reflect on these alternate histories, we are reminded of the value of curiosity, critical thinking, and open-mindedness. By considering how different decisions could have led to different outcomes, we become more aware of the potential for change and innovation in our own world. This imaginative exploration can inspire us to strive for a better future, informed by the lessons of the past.

Encouragement to Explore and Question History

One of the key takeaways from this journey through alternate histories is the importance of exploring and questioning our understanding of history. History is not just a series of dates and events;

it is a dynamic and evolving narrative shaped by the perspectives and interpretations of those who study it.

By questioning and reimagining historical events, we open ourselves to new insights and possibilities. This process of exploration encourages us to look beyond the established narratives and consider the broader context and underlying causes of historical events. It also helps us recognize the agency of individuals and communities in shaping their destinies.

We should approach history with a sense of curiosity and a willingness to challenge our assumptions. By doing so, we can develop a more nuanced and comprehensive understanding of the past, which in turn can inform our actions and decisions in the present.

Final Thoughts

As we conclude our journey through these fifteen alternate histories, it is important to remember that the exploration of "what if" scenarios is not just an intellectual exercise. It is a way to honor the complexities of history and the myriad factors that have shaped our world.

History is a tapestry woven from countless threads, each representing a different event, decision, or individual. By pulling on these threads and imagining how they might have been woven differently, we gain a greater appreciation for the richness and diversity of our shared human experience.

The study of alternate histories reminds us that the future is not fixed; it is shaped by the choices we make today. As we move forward, let us carry with us the lessons learned from these imagined pasts and use them to guide our actions and decisions. By embracing the power of imagination, critical thinking, and open-mindedness, we can create a future that is both informed by history and inspired by the possibilities of what could be.

In closing, I encourage you to continue exploring history with curiosity and imagination. Question the narratives, seek out new perspectives, and consider the "what ifs" that lie within the pages of our past. By doing so, you will not only deepen your understanding of history but also contribute to the ongoing story of humanity, one that is ever-evolving and full of potential.

## *About the Author*

David Reece was born 1999 in Las Vegas, Nevada were he attended UNLV. He now lives in New Orleans with his wife Trudy and their two boys Bruce & Tommy. He is the author of several books written for kids in junior high and 3 technical manuals with one specializing The Art of Horse Racing.

His passion for writing is only exceeded by his love for children and often speaks at schools and other events about how even youngsters can start writing at a young age.

He has been often praised for the positive messages his books put out.